WOLFSHEAD

BY

ROBERT E. HOWARD

British Library Cataloguing-in-Publication Data
A catalogue record for this book is available from the
British Library

Robert E. Howard

Robert Ervin Howard was born in Peaster, Texas in 1906. During his youth, his family moved between a variety of Texan boomtowns, and Howard – a bookish and somewhat introverted child – was steeped in the violent myths and legends of the Old South. Although he loved reading and learning, Howard developed a distinctly Texan, hardboiled outlook on the world. He became a passionate fan of boxing, taking it up at an amateur level, and from the age of nine began to write adventure tales of semi-historical bloodshed. In 1919, when Howard was thirteen, his family moved to the Central Texas hamlet of Cross Plains, where he would stay for the rest of his life.

At fifteen Howard began to read the pulp magazines of the day, and to write more seriously. The December 1922 issue of his high school newspaper featured two of his stories, 'Golden Hope Christmas' and 'West is West'. In 1924 he sold his first piece – a short caveman tale titled 'Spear and Fang' – for $16 to the not-yet-famous *Weird Tales* magazine. He published with the magazine regularly over the next few years. 1929 was a breakout year for Howard, in that the 23-year-old writer began to sell to other magazines, such as *Ghost Stories* and *Argosy*, both of whom had previously sent him hundreds of rejection slips. In 1930, he began a correspondence with weird fiction master H. P. Lovecraft which ran up to his death six years later, and is regarded as one of the great correspondence cycles in all of fantasy literature.

It was partly due to Lovecraft's encouragement that Howard created his most famous character, Conan the Cimmerian. Conan – a barbarian-turned-King during the Hyborian Age, a mythical period of some 12,000 years ago – featured in seventeen *Weird Tales* stories between 1933 and 1936, and is now regarded as having spawned the 'sword and sorcery' genre, making Howard's influence on fantasy literature comparable to that of J. R. R. Tolkien's. The Conan stories have since been adapted many times, most famously in the series of films starring Arnold Schwarzenegger.

Howard was enjoying an all-time high in sales by the beginning of 1936, but he was also deeply upset by the ill health of his mother, who had fallen into a coma. On the morning of June 11, 1936, he asked an attending nurse whether she would ever recover, and the nurse replied negatively. Howard walked to his car, parked outside the family home in Cross Plains, and shot himself. He died eight hours later, aged just thirty.

Fear? your pardon, Messieurs, but the meaning of fear you do not know. No, I hold to my statement. You are soldiers, adventurers. You have known the charges of regiments of dragoons, the frenzy of wind-lashed seas. But fear, real hair-raising, horror-crawling fear, you have not known. I myself have known such fear; but until the legions of darkness swirl from hell's gate and the world flames to ruin, will never such fear again be known to men:

Hark, I will tell you the tale; for it was many years ago and half across the world; and none of you will ever see the man of whom I tell you, or seeing, know.

Return, then, with me across the years to a day when I; a reckless young cavalier, stepped from the small boat that had landed me from the ship floating in the harbor, cursed the mud that littered the crude wharf, and strode up the landing toward the castle, in answer to the invitation of an old friend, Dom Vincente da Lusto.

Dom Vincente was a strange, far-sighted man-a strong man, one who saw visions beyond the ken of his time. In his veins, perhaps, ran the blood of those old Phoenicians who, the priests tell us, ruled the seas and built cities in far lands, in the dim ages. His plan of fortune was strange and yet successful; few men would have thought of it; fewer could have succeeded. For his estate was upon the western coast

of that dark, mystic continent, that baffler of explorers--
Africa.

There by a small bay had he cleared away the sullen
jungle, built his castle and his storehouses, and with ruthless
hand had he wrested the riches of the land. Four ships he
had: three smaller craft and one great galleon. These plied
between his domains and the cities of Spain, Portugal,
France, and even England, laden with rare woods, ivory,
slaves; the thousand strange riches that Dom Vincente had
gained by trade and by conquest.

Aye, a wild venture, a wilder commerce. And yet might
he have shaped an empire from the dark land, had it not
been for the rat-faced Carlos, his nephew-but I run ahead
of my tale.

Look, Messieurs, I draw a map on the table, thus, with
finger dipped in wine. Here lay the small, shallow harbor, and
here the wide wharves: A landing ran thus, up the slight slope
with hutlike warehouses on each side, and here it stopped at
a wide, shallow moat. Over it went a--narrow drawbridge
and then one was confronted with a high palisade of logs set
in the ground. This extended entirely around the castle. The
castle itself was built on the model of another, earlier age;
being more for strength than beauty. Built of stone brought
from a great distance; years of labor and a thousand Negroes
toiling--beneath the lash had reared its walls, and now,
completely, it offered an almost impregnable appearance.

4

Such was the--intention of its builders, for Barbary pirates ranged the coasts, and the horror of a native uprising lurked ever near.

A space of about a half-mile on every side of the castle was kept cleared away and roads had been built through the marshy land. All this had required an immense amount of labor, but manpower was plentiful. A present to a chief, and he furnished all that was needed, And Portuguese know how to make men work!

Less than three hundred yards to the east of the castle ran a wide, shallow river, which emptied into the harbor. The name has entirely slipt my mind. It was a heathenish title and I could never lay my tongue to it.

I found that I was not the only friend invited to the castle. It seems that once a year or some such matter, Dom Vincente brought a host of jolly companions to his lonely estate and made merry for some weeks, to make up for the work and solitude of the rest of the year.

In fact, it was nearly night, and a great banquet was in progress when I entered. I was acclaimed with great delight, greeted boisterously by friends and introduced to such strangers as were there.

Entirely too weary to take much part in the revelry, I ate, drank quietly, listened to the toasts and songs, and studied the feasters.

Dom Vincente, of course, I knew, as I had been intimate with him for years; also his pretty niece, Ysabel, who was one reason I had accepted his invitation to come to that stinking wilderness. Her second cousin, Carlos, I knew and disliked-a sly, mincing fellow with a face like a mink's. Then there was my old friend, Luigi Verenza, an Italian; and his flirt of a sister, Marcita, making eyes at the men as usual. Then there was a short, stocky German who called himself Baron von Scluller; and Jean Desmarte, an out-at-the-elbows nobleman of Gascony; and Don Florenzo de Seville, a lean, dark, silent man, who called himself a Spaniard and wore a rapier nearly as long as himself.

There were others, men and women, but it was long ago and all their names and faces I do not remember. But there was one man whose face somehow drew my gaze as an alchemist's magnet draws steel. He was a leanly built man of slightly more than medium height, dressed plainly, almost austerely, and he wore a sword almost as long as the Spaniard's.

But it was neither his clothes nor his sword which attracted my attention. It was his face. A refined, high-bred face, it was furrowed deep with lines that gave it a weary, haggard expression. Tiny scars flecked jaw and forehead as if torn by savage claws; I could have sworn the narrow gray eyes had a fleeting, haunted look in their expression at times.

I leaned over to that flirt, Marcita, and asked the name of the man, as it had slipt my mind that we had been introduced.

"De Montour, from Normandy," she answered. "A strange man. I don't think I like him."

"Then he resists your snares, my little enchantress?" I murmured; long friendship making me as immune from her anger as from her wiles. But she chose not to be angry and answered coyly, glancing from under demurely lowered lashes.

I watched de Montour much, feeling somehow a strange fascination. He ate lightly, drank much, seldom spoke, and then only to answer questions.

Presently, toasts making the rounds, I noticed his companions urging him to rise and give a health. At first he refused, then rose, upon their repeated urgings, and stood silent for a moment, goblet raised. He seemed to dominate, to overawe the group of revelers. Then with a mocking, savage laugh, he lifted the goblet above his head.

"To Solomon," he exclaimed, "who bound all devils! And thrice cursed be he for that some escaped!"

A toast and a curse in one! It was drunk silently, and with many sidelong, doubting glances.

That night I retired early, weary of the long sea voyage and my head spinning from the strength of the wine,--of which Dom Vincente kept such great stores.

My room was near the top of the castle and looked out toward the forests of the south and the river. The room was furnished in crude, barbaric splendor, as was all the rest of the castle.

Going to the window, I gazed out at the arquebusier pacing the castle grounds just inside the palisade; at the cleared space lying unsightly and barren in the moonlight; at the forest beyond; at the silent river.

From the native quarters close to the river bank came the weird twanging of some rude lute, sounding a barbaric melody.

In the dark shadows of the forest some uncanny nightbird lifted a mocking voice. A thousand minor notes sounded-birds, and beasts, and the devil knows what else! Some great jungle cat began a hair-lifting yowling. I shrugged my shoulders and turned from the windows. Surely devils lurked in those somber depths.

There came a knock at my door and I opened it, to, admit de Montour.

He strode to the window and gazed at the moon, which rode resplendent and glorious.

"The moon is almost full, is it not, Monsieur?" he remarked, turning to me. I nodded, and I could have sworn that he shuddered.

"Your pardon, Monsieur. I will not annoy you further."
He turned to go, but at the door turned and retraced his
steps.

"Monsieur," he almost whispered, with a fierce
intensity, "whatever you do, be sure you bar and bolt your
door tonight!"

Then he was gone, leaving me to stare after him
bewilderedly.

I dozed off to sleep, the distant shouts of the revelers
in my ears, and though I was weary, or perhaps because of
it, I slept lightly. While I never really awoke until morning,
sounds and noises seemed to drift to me through my veil of
slumber, and once it seemed that something was prying and
shoving against the bolted door.

As is to be supposed, most of the guests were in a
beastly humor the following day and remained in their
rooms most of the morning or else straggled down late.
Besides Dom Vincente there were really only three of the
masculine members sober: de Montour; the Spaniard, de
Seville (as he called himself); and myself. The Spaniard never
touched wine, and though de Montour consumed incredible
quantities of it, it never affected him in any way.

The ladies greeted us most graciously.

"S'truth, Signor," remarked that minx Marcita, giving
me her hand with a gracious air that was like to make me
snicker, "I am glad to see there are gentlemen among us who

care more for our company than for the wine cup; for most of them are most surprizingly befuddled this morning."

Then with a most outrageous turning of her wondrous eyes, "Methinks someone was too drunk to be discreet last night--or not drunk enough. For unless my poor senses deceive me much, someone came fumbling at my door late in the night."

"Ha!" I exclaimed in quick anger, "some-!"

"No. Hush." She glanced about as if to see that we were alone, then: "Is it not strange that Signor de Montour, before he retired last night, instructed me to fasten my door firmly?"

"Strange," I murmured, but did not tell her that he had told me the same thing.

"And is it not strange, Pierre, that though Signor de Montour left the banquet hall even before you did, yet he has the appearance of one who has been up all night?" I shrugged. A woman's fancies are often strange.

"Tonight," she said roguishly, "I will leave my door unbolted and see whom I catch."

"You will do no such thing."

She showed her little teeth in a contemptuous smile and displayed a small, wicked dagger.

"Listen, imp. De Montour gave me: the same warning he did you. Whatever he knew, whoever prowled the halls last night, the object was more apt murder than amorous adventure. Keep you your doors bolted. The lady Ysabel shares your room, does she not?"

"Not she. And I send my woman to the slave quarters at night," she murmured, gazing mischievously at me from beneath drooping eyelids..

"One would think you a girl of no character from your talk," I told her, with the frankness of youth and of long friendship. "Walk with care, young lady, else I tell your brother to spank you."

And I walked away to pay my respects to Ysabel. The Portuguese girl was the very opposite of Marcita, being a shy, modest young thing, not so beautiful as the Italian, but exquisitely pretty in an appealing, almost childish air. I once had thoughts-Hi ho! To be young and foolish!

Your pardon, Messieurs. An old man's mind wanders. It was of de Montour that I meant to tell you--de Montour and Dom Vincente's mink-faced cousin.

A band of armed natives were thronged about the gates, kept at a distance by the Portuguese soldiers. Among them were some score of young men and women all naked, chained neck to neck. Slaves they were, captured by some warlike tribe and brought for sale. Dom Vincente looked them over personally.

Followed a long haggling and bartering, of which I quickly wearied and turned away, wondering that a man of

Dom Vincente's rank could so demean himself as to stoop to trade.

But I strolled back when one of the natives of the village nearby came up and interrupted the sale with a long harangue to Dom Vincente.

While they talked de Montour came up, and presently Dom Vincente turned to us and said, "One of the woodcutters of the village was torn to pieces by a leopard or some such beast last night. A strong young man and unmarried."

"A leopard? Did they, see it?" suddenly asked de Montour, and when Dom Vincente said no, that it came and went in the night, de Montour lifted a trembling hand and drew it across his forehead, as if to brush away cold sweat.

"Look you, Pierre," quoth Dom Vincente, "I have here a slave who, wonder of wonders, desires to be your man. Though the devil only knows why."

He led up a slim young Jakri, a mere youth, whose main asset seemed a merry grin.

"He is yours," said Dom Vincente. "He is goodly trained and will make a fine servant. And look ye, a slave is of an advantage over a servant, for all he requires is food and a loincloth or so with a touch of the whip to keep him in his place."

It was not long before. I learned why Gola wished to be "my man," choosing me among all the rest. It was because of my hair. Like many dandies of that day, I. wore it long and curled, the strands falling to my shoulders. As it happened, I was the only man of the party who so wore my hair, and Gola would sit and gaze at it in silent admiration for hours at a time, or until, growing nervous under his unblinking scrutiny, I would boot him forth.

It was that night that a brooding animosity, hardly apparent, between Baron von Schiller and Jean Desmarie broke out into a flame.

As usual, woman was the cause. Marcita carried-on a most outrageous flirtation with both of them.

That was not wise. Desmarte was a wild young fool. Von Schiller was a lustful beast. But when, Messieurs, did woman ever use wisdom?

Their hate flamed to a murderous fury when the German sought to kiss Marcita.

Swords were clashing in an instant. But before Dom Vincente could thunder a command to halt, Luigi was between the combatants, and had beaten their swords down, hurling them back viciously.

"Signori," said he softly, but with a fierce intensity, "is it the part of high-bred signori to fight over my sister? Ha, by the toenails of Satan, for the toss of a coin I would call you both out! You, Marcita, go to your chamber, instantly, nor leave until I give you permission."

And she went, for, independent though she was, none cared to face the slim, effeminate-appearing youth when a tigerish snarl curled his lips, a murderous gleam lightened his dark eyes.

Apologies were made, but from the glances the two rivals threw at each other, we knew that the quarrel was not forgotten and would blaze forth again at the slightest pretext.

Late that night I woke suddenly with a strange, eery feeling of horror. Why, I could not say. I rose, saw that the door was firmly bolted, and seeing Gola asleep art the floor, kicked him awake irritably.

And just as he got up, hastily, rubbing himself, the silence was broken by a wild scream, a scream that rang through the castle and brought a startled shout from the arquebusier pacing the palisade; a scream from the mouth of a girl, frenzied with terror.

Gola squawked and dived behind the divan. I jerked the door open and raced down the dark corridor. Dashing down a winding stair, I caromed into someone at the bottom and we tumbled headlong.

He rasped something and I recognized the voice of Jean Desmarte. I hauled him to his feet, and raced along, he following; the screams had ceased, but the whole castle was in an uproar, voices shouting, the clank of weapons, lights flashing up, Dom Vincente's voice shouting for the soldiers, the noise of armed men rushing through the rooms and falling over each other. With all the confusion, Desmarte, the Spaniard, and I reached Marcita's room just as Luigi darted inside and snatched his sister into his arms.

Others rushed in, carrying lights and weapons, shouting, demanding to know what was occurring.

The girl lay quietly in her brother's arms, her dark hair loose and rippling over her shoulders, her dainty night-garments torn to shreds and exposing her lovely body. Long scratches showed upon her arms, breasts and shoulders.

Presently, she opened her eyes, shuddered, then shrieked wildly and clung frantically to Luigi, begging him not to let something take her.

"The door!" she whimpered. "I left it unbarred. And something crept into my room through the darkness. I struck at it with my dagger and it hurled me to the floor, tearing, tearing at me. Then I fainted."

"Where is von Schiller?" asked the Spaniard, a fierce glint in his dark eyes. Every man glanced at his neighbor. All the guests were there except the German. I noted de Montour gazing at the terrified girl, his face more haggard than usual. And I thought it strange that he wore no weapon.

"Aye, von Schiller!" exclaimed Desmarte fiercely. And half of us followed Dom Vincente out into the corridor. We began a vengeful search through the castle, and in a small, dark hallway we found von Schiller. On his face he lay, in a crimson, ever-widening stain.

"This is the work of some native!" exclaimed Desmarte, face aghast.

"Nonsense," bellowed Dom Vincente. "No native from the outside could pass the soldiers. All slaves, von Schiller's among them, were barred and bolted in the slave quarters, except Cola, who sleeps in Pierre's room, and Ysabel's woman."

"But who else could have done this deed?" exclaimed Desmarte in a fury.

"You!" I said abruptly; "else why ran you so swiftly away from the room of Marcita?"

"Curse you, you lie!" he shouted, and his swift-drawn sword leaped for my breast; but quick as he was, the Spaniard was quicker. Desmarte's rapier clattered against the wall and Desmarte stood like a statue, the Spaniard's motionless point just touching his throat.

"Bind him," said the Spaniard without passion. "Put down your blade, Don Florenzo," commanded Dom Vincente, striding forward and dominating the scene. "Signor Desmarte, you are one of my best friends, but I am the only law here and duty must be done. Give your word that you will not seek to escape."

"I give it," replied the Gascon calmly. "I acted hastily. I apologize. I was not intentionally running away, but the halls and corridors of this cursed castle confuse me." Of us all, probably but one man believed him.

"Messieurs!" De Montour stepped forward. "This youth is not guilty. Turn the German over."

Two soldiers did as he asked. De Montour shuddered, pointing. The rest of us glanced once, then recoiled in horror.

"Could man have done that thing?" "With a dagger--" began someone.

"No dagger makes wounds like that," said the Spaniard: "The German was torn to pieces by the talons of some frightful beast."

We glanced about us, half expecting some hideous monster to leap upon us from the shadows.

We searched that castle; every foot, every inch of it. And we found no trace of any beast.

Dawn was breaking when I returned to my room, to find that Gola had barred himself in; and it took me nearly a half-hour to convince him to let me in. Having smacked him soundly and berated him for his cowardice, I told him what had taken place, as he could understand French and: could speak a weird mixture which he proudly called French.

His mouth gaped and only the whites of his eyes showed as the tale reached its climax.

"Ju ju!" he whispered fearsomely. "Fetish man!" Suddenly an idea came to me. I had heard vague tales, little more than hints of legends, of the devilish leopard cult that existed on the West Coast. No white man had ever seen one of its votaries, but Dom Vincente had told us tales of beast-men, disguised in skins of leopards, who stole through the midnight jungle and slew and devoured. A ghastly thrill traveled up and down my spine, and in an instant I had Gola in a grasp which made him veil.

"Was that a leopard-man?" I hissed, shaking him viciously.

"Massa, massa!" he gasped. "Me good boy! Ju ju man Qet! More besser no tell!"

"You'll tell--me!" I gritted, renewing my endeavors, until, his hands waving feeble protests, he promised to tell me what he knew.

"No leopard-man!" he whispered, and his eyes grew big with supernatural fear. "Moon, he full, woodcutter find, him heap clawed. Find 'nother woodcutter. Big Massa (Dom Vincente) say, 'leopard.' No leopard. But leopard-man, he come to kill. Something kill leopardman! Heap claw! Hai, hai! Moon full again. Something come in, lonely hut; claw um woman, claw um pick'nin. I an find um claw up. Big Massa say 'leopard..' Full moon again, and woodcutter find, heap clawed. Now come in castle. No leopard. But always footmarks of a man'."

I gave a startled, incredulous exclamation.

It was true, Gola averred. Always the footprints of a man led away from the scene of the murder. Then why did the natives not tell the Big Massa that he might hunt down the fiend? Here Gala assumed a crafty expression and whispered in my ear, The footprints were of a man who wore shoes!

Even assuming that Gola was lying, I felt a thrill of unexplainable horror. Who, then, did the natives believe was doing these frightful murders?

And he answered: Dom Vincente!

By this time, Messieurs, my mind was in a whirl. What was the meaning of all this? Who stew the German and sought to ravish Marcita? And as I reviewed the crime, it appeared to me that murder rather than rape was the object of the attack.

Why did de Montour warn us, and then appear to have knowledge of the crime, telling us that Desmarte was innocent and then proving it?

It was all beyond me.

The tale of the slaughter got among the natives, in spite of all we could do, and they appeared restless and nervous, and thrice that day Dom Vincente had a black lashed for insolence. A brooding atmosphere pervaded the castle.

I considered going to Dom Vincente with Gola's tale, but decided to wait awhile.

The women kept their chambers that, day, the men were restless and moody. Dom Vincente announced that the sentries would be doubled and some would patrol the corridors of the castle itself. I found myself musing cynically that if Gola's suspicions were true, sentries would be of little good.

I am not, Messieurs, a man to brook such a situation with patience. And I was young then. So as we drank before retiring, I flung my goblet on the table and angrily announced that in spite of man, beast or devil, I slept that night with doors flung wide. And I tramped angrily to my chamber.

Again, as on the first night, de Montour came. And his face was as a man who has looked into the gaping gates of hell.

"I have come," he said, "to ask you--nay, Monsieur, to implore you-to reconsider your rash determination." I shook my head impatiently..

"You are resolved? Yes? Then I ask you do to this for me, that after I enter my chamber, you will bolt my doors from the outside."

I did as he asked, and then made my way back to my chamber, my mind in a maze of wonderment. I had sent Gola to the slave quarters, and I laid rapier and dagger close at hand. Nor did I go to bed, but crouched in a great chair, in the darkness. Then I had much ado to keep from sleeping. To keep myself awake, I fell to musing on the strange words of de Montour. He seemed to be laboring under great excitement; his eyes hinted of ghastly mysteries known to him alone. And yet his face was not that of a wicked man.

Suddenly the notion took me to go to his chamber and talk with him.

Walking those dark passages was a shuddersome task, but eventually I stood before de Montour's door. I called softly. Silence. I reached out a hand and felt splintered fragments of wood. Hastily I struck flint and steel which I carried, and the flaming tinder showed the great oaken door sagging on its mighty hinges; showed a door smashed and splintered from the inside: And the chamber of de Montour was unoccupied.

Some instinct prompted me to hurry back to my room, swiftly but silently, shoeless feet treading softly. And as I neared the door, I was aware of something in the darkness before me. Something which crept in from a side corridor and glided stealthily along.

In a wild panic of, fear I leaped, striking wildly and aimlessly in the darkness. All my clenched fist encountered a human head, and something went down with a crash. Again I struck a light; a man lay senseless on the floor, and he was de Montour.

I thrust a candle into a niche in the Wall, and just then de Montour's eyes opened and he rose uncertainly. "You!" I exclaimed, hardly knowing what I said. "You, of all men!"

He merely nodded.

"You killed von Schiller?"

"Yes."

I recoiled with a gasp of horror.

"Listen." He raised his hand. "Take your rapier and run me through. No man will touch you."

"No," I exclaimed. "I can not."

"Then, quick," he said hurriedly, "get into your chamber and bolt the door. Haste! It will return!"

"What will return?" I asked, with a thrill of horror. "If it will harm me, it will harm you. Come into the chamber with me."

"No, no!" he fairly shrieked, springing back from my outstretched arm. "Haste, haste! It left me for an instant, but it will return." Then in a low-pitched voice of indescribable horror: "It is returning. It is here now!"

And I felt a something, a formless, shapeless presence near. A thing of frightfulness.

De Montour was standing, legs braced, arms thrown back, fists clenched. The muscles bulged beneath his skin, his eyes widened and narrowed, the veins stood out upon his forehead as if in great physical effort. As I looked, to my horror, out of nothing, a shapeless, nameless something took vague form! Like a shadow it moved upon de Montour.

It was hovering about him! Good God, it was merging, becoming one with the man!

De Montour swayed; a great gasp escaped him. The dim thing vanished. De Montour wavered. Then he turned toward me, and may God grant that I never look on a face like that again!

It was a hideous, a bestial face. The eyes gleamed with a frightful ferocity; the snarling lips were drawn back from gleaming teeth, which to my startled gaze appeared more like bestial fangs than human teeth.

Silently the thing (I can not call it a human) slunk toward me. Gasping with horror I sprang back and through the door, just as the thing launched itself through the air, with a sinuous motion which even then made me think of a leaping wolf. I slammed the door, holding it against the frightful thing which hurled itself again and again against it.

Finally it desisted and I heard it slink stealthily off down the corridor. Faint and exhausted I sat down, waiting, listening. Through the open window wafted the breeze, bearing all the scents of Africa, the spicy and the foul. From the native village came the sound of a native drum. Other drums answered farther up the river and back in the bush. Then from somewhere in the jungle, horridly incongruous, sounded the long, high-pitched call of a timber wolf. My soul revolted.

Dawn brought a tale of terrified villagers, of a Negro woman torn by some fiend of the night, barely escaping. And to de Montour I went:

On the way I met Dom Vincente: He was perplexed and angry.

"Some hellish thing is at work in this castle," he said. "Last night, though I have said naught of it to anyone, something leaped upon the back of one of the arquebusiers, tore the leather jerkin from his shoulders and pursued him to the barbican. More, someone locked de Montour into his room last night, and he was forced to smash the door to get out."

He strode on, muttering to himself, and I proceeded down the stairs, more puzzled than ever.

De Montour sat upon a stool, gazing out the window. An indescribable air of weariness was about him.

His long hair was uncombed and tousled, his garments were tattered. With a shudder I saw faint crimson stains upon his hands,-and noted that the nails were torn and broken.

He looked up as I came in, and waved me to a seat. His face was worn and haggard, but was that of a man.

After a moment's silence, he spoke.

"I will tell you my strange tale. Never before has it passed my lips, and why I tell you, knowing that you will not believe me, I can not say."

And then I listened to what was surely the wildest, the most fantastic, the weirdest tale ever heard by man.

"Years ago," said de Montour, "I was upon a military mission in northern France. Alone, I was forced to pass through the fiend haunted woodlands of Villefere. In those frightful forests I was beset by an inhuman, a ghastly thing-a werewolf. Beneath a midnight moon we fought, and slew it. Now this is the truth: that if a werewolf is slain in the half-form of a man, its ghost will haunt its slayer through eternity. But if it is slain as a wolf, hell gapes to receive it. The true werewolf is not (as many think) a man who may take the form of a wolf, but a wolf who takes the form of a man!

"Now listen, my friend, and I will tell you of the wisdom, the hellish knowledge that is mine, gained through many a frightful deed, imparted to me amid the ghastly shadows of midnight forests where fiends and half-beasts roamed.

"In the beginning, the world was strange, misshapen. Grotesque beasts wandered through its jungles. Driven from another world, ancient demons and fiends came in great numbers and settled upon this newer, younger world. Long the forces of good and evil warred.

"A strange beast, known as man, wandered among the other beasts, and since good or bad must have a concrete form ere either accomplishes its desire, the spirits of good entered man. The fiends entered other beasts, reptiles and birds; and long and fiercely waged the age-old battle. But man conquered. The great dragons and serpents were slain and with them the demons. Finally, Solomon, wise beyond the ken of man, made great war upon them, and by virtue of his wisdom, slew, seized and bound. But there were some which were the fiercest, the boldest, and though Solomon drove them out he could not conquer them. Those had taken the form of wolves. As the ages passed, wolf and demon became merged. No longer could the fiend leave the body of the wolf at will. In many instances, the savagery of the wolf overcame the subtlety of the demon and enslaved him, so the wolf became again only a beast, a fierce, cunning beast, but merely a beast. But of the werewolves, there are many, even yet."

"And during the time of the full moon, the wolf may take the form, or the half-form of a man. When the moon hovers at her zenith, however, the wolf-spirit again takes ascendency and the werewolf becomes a true wolf once more. But if it is slain in the form of a man, then the spirit is free to haunt its slayer through the ages."

"Harken now. I had thought to have slain the thing after it had changed to its true shape. But I slew it an instant too soon. The moon, though it approached the zenith, had not yet reached it, nor had the thing taken on fully the wolf-form."

"Of this I knew nothing and went my way. But when the neat time approached for the full moon, I began to be aware of a strange, malicious influence. An atmosphere of horror hovered in the air and I was aware of inexplicable, uncanny impulses.

"One night in a small village in the center of a great forest, the influence came upon me with full power. It was night, and the moon, nearly full, was rising over the forest. And between the moon and me, I saw, floating in the upper air, ghostly and barely discernible, the outline of a wolf's head!

"I remember little of what happened thereafter. I remember, dimly, clambering into the silent street, remember struggling, resisting briefly, vainly, and the rest is a crimson maze, until I came to myself the next morning and found my garments and hands caked and stained crimson; and heard the horrified chattering of the villagers, telling of a pair of clandestine lovers, slaughtered in a ghastly manner, scarcely outside the village, torn to pieces as if by wild beasts, as if by wolves.

"From that village I fled aghast, but I fled not alone. In the day I could not feel the drive of my fearful captor, but when night fell and the moon rose, I ranged the silent forest, a frightful-thing, a slayer of humans, a fiend in a man's body.

"God, the battles I have fought! But always it overcame me and drove me ravening after some new victim. But after the moon had passed its fullness, the thing's power over me ceased suddenly. Nor did it return until three nights before the moon was full again.

"Since then I have roamed the world-fleeing, fleeing, seeking to escape. Always the thing follows, taking possession of my body when the moon is full. Gods, the frightful deeds I have done!

"I would have slain myself long ago, but I dare not. For the soul of a suicide is accurst, and my soul would be forever hunted through the flames of hell. And harken, most frightful of all, my slain body would for ever roam the earth, moved and inhabited by the soul of the werewolf! Can any thought be more ghastly?

"And I seem immune to the weapons of man. Swords have pierced me, daggers have hacked me. I am covered with scars. Yet never have they struck me down. In Germany they bound and led me to the block. There would I have willingly placed my head, but the thing came upon me, and breaking my bonds, I slew and fled. Up and down the world I have wandered, leaving horror and slaughter in my trail. Chains, cells, can not hold me. The thing is fastened to me through all eternity.

"In desperation I accepted Dom Vincente's invitation, for look you, none knows of my frightful double life, since no one could recognize me in the clutch of the demon; and few, seeing me, live to tell of it.

"My hands are red, my soul doomed to everlasting flames, my mind is torn with remorse for my crimes. And yet I can do nothing to help myself. Surely, Pierre, no man ever knew the hell that I have known.

"Yes, I slew von Schiller, and I sought, to destroy the girl Marcita. Why I did not, I can not say, for I have slain both women and men.

"Now, if you will, take your sword and slay me, and with my last breath I will give you the good God's blessing. No?

"You know now my tale and you see before you a man, fiend-haunted for all eternity."

My mind was spinning with wonderment as I left the room of de Montour. What to do, I knew not. It seemed likely that he would yet murder us all, and yet I could not bring myself to tell Dom Vincente all. From the bottom of my soul I pitied de Montour.

So I kept my peace, and in the days that followed I made occasion to seek him out and converse with him. A real friendship sprang up between us.

About this time that black devil, Gola, began to wear an air of suppressed excitement, as if he knew something he wished desperately to tell, but would not or else dared not.

So the days passed in feasting, drinking and hunting, until one night de Montour came to my chamber and pointed silently at the moon which was just rising.

"Look ye," he said, "I have a plan. I will give it out that I am going into the jungle for hunting and will go forth, apparently for several days. But at night I will return to the castle, and you must lock me into the dungeon which is used as a storeroom."

This we did, and I managed to slip down twice a day and carry food and drink to my friend. He insisted on remaining in the dungeon even in the day, for though the fiend had never exerted its influence over him in the daytime, and he believed it powerless then, yet he would take no chances.

It was during this time that I began to notice that Dom Vincente's mink-faced cousin, Carlos, was forcing his attentions upon Ysabel, who was his second cousin, and who seemed to resent those attentions.

Myself, I would have challenged him for a duel for the toss of a coin, for I despised him, but it was really none of my affair. However, it seemed that Ysabel feared him.

My friend Luigi, by the way, had become enamored of the dainty Portuguese girl, and was making swift love to her daily.

And de Montour sat in his cell and reviewed his ghastly deeds until he battered the bars with his bare hands.

And Don Florenzo wandered about the castle grounds like a dour Mephistopheles.

And the other guests rode and quarreled and drank.

And Gola slithered about, eyeing me if always on the point of imparting momentous information. What wonder if my nerves became rasped to the shrieking point?

Each day the natives grew surlier and more and more sullen and intractable.

One night, not long before the full of the moon, I entered the dungeon where de Montour sat.

He looked up quickly.

"You dare much, coming to me in the night."

I shrugged my shoulders, seating myself.

A small barred window let in the night scents and sounds of Africa.

"Hark to the native drums," I said. "For the past week they have sounded almost incessantly."

De Montour assented.

"The natives are restless. Methinks 'tis deviltry they are planning. Have you noticed that Carlos is much among them?"

"No," I answered, "but 'tis like there will be a break between him and Luigi. Luigi is paying court to Ysabel."

So we talked, when suddenly de Montour became silent and moody, answering only in monosyllables.

The moon rose and peered in at the barred windows. De Montour's face was illuminated by its beams.

And then the hand of horror grasped me. On the wall behind de Montour appeared a shadow, a shadow clearly defined of a wolf's head!

At the same instant de Montour felt its influence. With a shriek he bounded from his stool.

He pointed fiercely, and as with trembling hands I slammed and bolted the door behind me, I felt him hurl his weight against it. As I fled up the stairway I heard a wild raving and battering at the iron-bound door. But with all the werewolf's might the great door held.

As I entered my room, Gola dashed in and gasped out the tale he had been keeping for days.

I listened, incredulously, and then dashed forth to find Dom Vincente.'

I was told that Carlos had asked him to accompany him to the village to arrange a sale of slaves.

My informer was Don Florenzo of Seville, and when I gave him a brief outline of Gola's tale; he accompanied me.

Together we dashed through the castle gate, flinging a word to the guards, and down the landing toward the village.

Dom Vincente, Dom Vincente, walk with care, keep sword loosened in its sheath! Fool, fool, to walk in the night with Carlos, the traitor!

They were nearing the village when we caught up with them. "Dom Vincente!" I exclaimed; "return instantly to the castle. Carlos is selling you into the hands of the natives! Gola has told me that he lusts for your wealth and for Ysabel! A terrified native babbled to him of booted footprints near the places where the woodcutters were murdered, and Carlos has made the blacks believe that the slayer was you! Tonight the natives were to rise and slay every man in the castle except Carlos! Do you not believe me, Dom Vincente?"

"Is this the truth, Carlos?" asked Dom Vincente, in amaze.

Carlos laughed mockingly.

"The fool speaks truth," he said, "but it accomplishes you nothing. Ho!"

He shouted as he leaped for Dom Vincente. Steel flashed in the moonlight and the Spaniard's sword was through Carlos ere he could move.

And the shadows rose about us. Then it was back to back, sword and dagger, three men against a hundred. Spears flashed, and a fiendish yell went up from savage throats. I spitted three natives in as many thrusts and then went down from a stunning swing from a warclub, and an instant later Dom Vincente fell upon me, with a spear in one arm and another through the leg. Don Florenzo was standing above us, sword leaping like a live thing, when a charge of the arquebusiers swept the river bank clear and we were borne into the castle.

The black hordes came with a rush, spears flashing like a wave of steel, a thunderous roar of savagery going up to the skies.

Time and again they swept up the slopes, bounding the moat, until they were swarming over the palisades. And time and again the fire of the hundred-odd defenders hurled them back.

They had set fire to the plundered warehouses, and their light vied with the light of the moon. Just across the river there was a larger storehouse, and about this hordes of the natives gathered, tearing it apart for plunder.

"Would that they would drop a torch upon it," said Dom Vincente, "for naught is stored therein save some thousand pounds of gunpowder. I dared not store the treacherous stuff this side of the river. All the tribes of the river and coast have gathered for our slaughter and all my ships are upon the seas. We may hold out awhile, but eventually they will swarm the palisade and put us to the slaughter."

I hastened to the dungeon wherein de Montour sat. Outside the door I called to him and he bade me enter in voice which told me the fiend had left him for an instant.

"The blacks have risen," I told him.

"I guessed as much. How goes the battle?"

I gave him the details of the betrayal and the fight, and mentioned the powder-house across the river. He sprang to his feet.

"Now by my hag-ridden soul!" he exclaimed. "I will fling the dice once more with hell! Swift, let me out of the castle! I will essay to swim the river and set off yon powder!"

"It is insanity!" I exclaimed. "A thousand blacks lurk between the palisades and the river, and thrice that number beyond! The' river itself swarms with crocodiles!"

"I will attempt it!" he answered, a great light in his face. "If I can reach it, some thousand natives will lighten the siege; if I am slain, then my soul is free and mayhap will gain some forgiveness for that I gave my life to atone for my crimes."

Then, "Haste," he exclaimed, "for the demon is returning! Already I feel his influence! Haste ye!"

For the castle gates we sped, and as de Montour ran he gasped as a man in a terrific battle.

At the gate he pitched headlong, then rose, to spring through it. Wild yells greeted him from the natives.

The arquebusiers shouted curses at him and at me. Peering down from the top of the palisades I saw him turn from side to side uncertainly. A score of natives were rushing recklessly forward, spears raised.

Then the eery wolf-yell rose to the skies, and de Montour bounded forward. Aghast, the natives paused, and before a man of them could move he was among them. Wild shrieks, not of rage, but of terror.

In amazement the arquebusiers held their fire.

Straight through the group of blacks de Montour charged, and when they broke and fled, three of them fled not.

A dozen steps de Montour took in pursuit; then stopped stock-still. A moment he stood so while spears flew about him, then turned and ran swiftly in the direction of the river.

A few steps from the river another band of blacks barred his way. In the famines light of the burning houses the scene was clearly illuminated. A thrown spear tore through de Montour's shoulder. Without pausing in his stride he tore it forth and drove it through a native, leaping over his body to get among the others. They could not face the fiend-driven white man. With shrieks they fled, and de Montour, bounding upon the' back of one, brought him down.

Then he rose, staggered and sprang to the river bank. An instant he paused there and then vanished in the shadows.

"Name of the devil!" gasped Dom Vincente at my shoulder. "What manner of man is that? Was that de Montour?"

I nodded. The wild yells of the natives rose above the crackle of the arquebus fire. They were massed thick about the great warehouse across the river.

"They plan a great rush," said Dom Vincente. "They will swarm clear over the palisade, methinks. Ha!"

A crash that seemed to rip the skies apart! A burst of flame that mounted to the stars! The castle rocked with the explosion. Then silence, as the smoke, drifting away, showed only a great crater where the warehouse had stood.

I could tell of how Dom Vincente led a charge, crippled as he was, out of the castle gate and, down the slope, to fall upon the terrified blacks who had escaped the explosion. I could tell of the slaughter, of the victory and the pursuit of the fleeing natives.

I could tell, too, Messieurs, of how I became separated from the band and of how I wandered far into the jungle, unable to find my way back to the coast.

I could tell how I was captured by a wandering band of slave raiders, and of how I escaped. But such is not my intention. In itself it would make a long tale; and it is of de Montour that I am speaking.

I thought much of the things that had passed and wondered if indeed de Montour reached the storehouse to blow it to the skies or whether it was but the deed of chance.

That a man could swim that reptile-swarming river, fiend-driven though he was, seemed impossible. And if he blew up the storehouse, he must have gone up with it.

So one night I pushed my way wearily through the jungle and sighted the coast, and close to the shore a small, tumbledown hut of thatch. To it I went, thinking to sleep therein if insects and reptiles would allow.

I entered the doorway and then stopped short. Upon a makeshift stool sat a man. He looked up as I entered and the rays of the moon fell across his face.

I started back with a ghastly thrill of horror. It was de Montour, and the moon was full!

Then as I stood, unable to flee, he rose and came toward me. And his face, though haggard as of a man who has looked into hell, was the face of a sane man.

"Come in, my friend," he said, and there was a great peace in his voice. "Come in and fear me not. The fiend has left me forever."

"But tell me, how conquered you?" I exclaimed as I grasped his hand.

"I fought a frightful battle, as I ran to the river," he answered, "for the fiend had me in its grasp and drove me to fall upon the natives. But for the first time my soul and mind gained ascendency for an instant, an instant just long enough to hold me to my purpose. And I believe the good saints came to my aid, for I was giving my life to save life.

"I leaped into the river and swam, and in an instant the crocodiles were swarming about me.

"Again in the clutch of the fiend I fought them, there in the river. Then suddenly the thing left me.

"I climbed from the river and fired the warehouse."

"The explosion hurled me hundreds of feet, and for days I wandered witless through the jungle."

"But the full moon came, and came again, and I felt not the influence of the fiend.

"I am free, free!" And a wondrous note of exultation, nay, exaltation, thrilled his words:

"My soul is free. Incredible as it seems, the demon lies drowned upon the bed of, the river, or else inhabits the body of one of the savage reptiles that swim the ways of the Niger."